Rocket
AND TH

Written by **Daniel Postgate**
Illustrated by **Pet Gotohda**

Published by Pearson Education Limited, Edinburgh Gate, Harlow, Essex, CM20 2JE
Registered company number: 872828

www.pearsonschools.co.uk

Text © Daniel Postgate 2011

Designed by Bigtop
Original illustrations © Pearson Education 2011
Illustrated by Pet Gotohda

The right of Daniel Postgate to be identified as author of this work has been asserted by him in accordance with the Copyright, Designs and Patents Act 1988.

First published 2011

15 14 13 12 11
10 9 8 7 6 5 4 3 2

British Library Cataloguing in Publication Data
A catalogue record for this book is available from the British Library

ISBN 978 0 435 91512 4

Printed and bound in Malaysia (CTP-VP)

Acknowledgements
We would like to thank the children and teachers of Bangor Central Integrated Primary School, NI; Bishop Henderson C of E Primary School, Somerset; Brookside Community Primary School, Somerset; Cheddington Combined School, Buckinghamshire; Cofton Primary School, Birmingham; Dair House Independent School, Buckinghamshire; Deal Parochial School, Kent; Newbold Riverside Primary School, Rugby and Windmill Primary School, Oxford for their invaluable help in the development and trialling of the Bug Club resources.

Every effort has been made to contact copyright holders of material reproduced in this book. Any omissions will be rectified in subsequent printings if notice is given to the publishers.

It was a fresh Spring morning and Veronica Witworth was in high spirits. She decided to ride her bike to school and maybe take a few minutes to ride around her favourite field on the way.

She set off up the road, turned onto the main street and pedalled for all she was worth.

Up ahead she saw a gloomy sight – a line of traffic at a standstill. Slamming on the brakes, she juddered to a halt and wondered what the hold-up was. She stood up on the pedals of her bike and peered over the line of cars. What she saw didn't please her at all, not one little bit. Traffic lights had been set up and large lorries and trucks were coming in and out of the field ahead – her favourite field.

She got off her bike and wheeled it along the pavement until she came to the traffic lights. A sign had been erected at the entrance to the field. It said:

New Development
Multi-storey car park being built.
Expect long delays.
We apologise for any inconvenience.

New D

Multi-storey

Exped

We apologise

This was far more than just an inconvenience for Veronica. It was an absolute disaster! This was her favourite field, with its grass and trees and flowers that she knew so well. She had played on it since she was old enough to walk. And it was being destroyed, just so that people could park their silly cars.

Just then, above the rumbling noise of the trucks, Veronica heard a bleeping sound. It was the contact console the Guardians had given her so that the space station, many hundreds of thousands of miles above Earth, could keep in touch. She took out the tiny, shiny little phone from her pocket and read the message on its screen:

EARTH
IS IN
DANGER!

"Quivering quasars!" Veronica exclaimed. "I had better get up to the space station fast!"

She locked her bike to a lamp post and looked for a place she could go where she wouldn't be seen. Eventually she found an alley between two houses and quickly nipped down it. Then, when she was sure nobody was looking, she pressed the red button on her contact console.

A moment later, she felt a tingling and a fizzing spread through her body. She shut her eyes tight as the rushing and roaring sound engulfed her, before mysteriously transporting her high into the sky, out of the atmosphere, and off into space.

When she opened her eyes she was standing at the centre of the space station, with its smooth white walls and twinkling lights. She was dressed in her space suit, complete with its jet-pack and helmet, ready for adventure. She was no longer just the schoolgirl Veronica Witworth. Now she was Rocket Ronnie – Defender of the Human Race!

"Welcome back, Rocket Ronnie," said a calm, cool voice in her ear. It was MAVIS, her on-board computer.

"It's nice to be back!" replied Rocket
Ronnie, with a grin. She heard a familiar
squeak and bleep and turned to see her
robotic friend and assistant, SID. He was
obviously very pleased to see Ronnie, and
he bobbed and rolled about in the air like
a berserk bouncing ball. "Hey, good to
see you too, SID," laughed Rocket Ronnie.
"So MAVIS, what's our impossible mission
for today?"

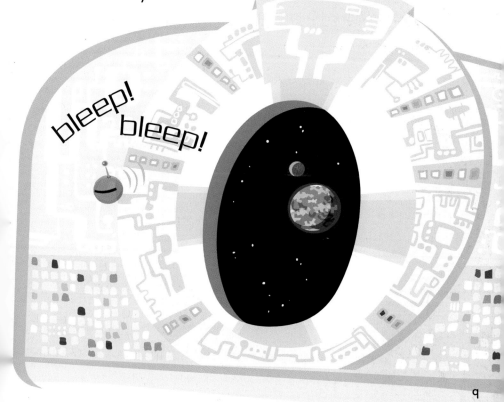

bleep!
bleep!

"This one is pretty tricky," said MAVIS, gravely. "Alien life forms have been detected by my sensors. They are in the solar system, but each time I try to locate their precise position, they seem to disappear. I don't know what they're up to. They might be perfectly harmless, but I need to find out. You must make contact with them and find out what they are doing here."

"OK," said Rocket Ronnie. "Sounds to me like a game of hide and seek, and I'm 'it'. I guess I had better get out there and start seeking. Are you coming, SID?" SID let out an enthusiastic, high-pitched whistle.

A panel in the wall of the station slid silently to one side and the vast, inky blackness of outer space lay spread out before them.

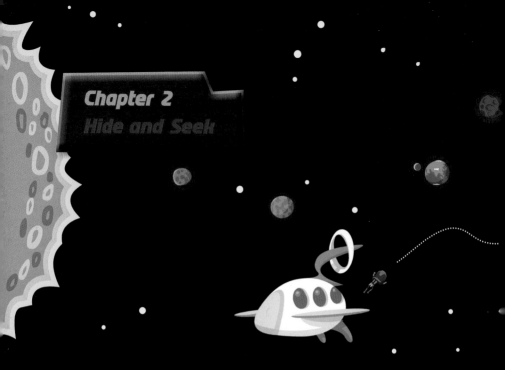

As Rocket Ronnie stepped off the floor of
the station, her jet-pack burst into life. Off
she went at a terrific speed, with her arms
held out in front of her and a huge smile
on her face. She enjoyed nothing better
than zooming though space. It was a
marvellous feeling.

"Hold on," she said, coming to a slow,
bobbing halt. "I don't know where I'm
going. MAVIS, where are these life forms
right now?"

"They seem to be somewhere near the rings of Saturn," replied MAVIS. *"I'll set up a location pointer for you."* A small red cross appeared on the screen of Rocket Ronnie's visor. All she had to do was keep the cross in the centre of the visor, then she would know that she was heading directly towards the life forms.

Rocket Ronnie blasted off again. Saturn was a very, very long way away so she had to go at a colossal speed. Poor SID had trouble keeping up. Eventually Rocket Ronnie and SID saw the magnificent planet of Saturn ahead of them.

"MAVIS, we're nearly there!" she said.
The little red cross suddenly swung to the
edge of her visor.

"The life forms have moved," said
MAVIS, calmly. *"They are now near the
planet Jupiter."*

"What?" exclaimed Rocket Ronnie.
"Shooting satellites! How did they get over
there so fast! OK, I'm on my way." She
swung round until the cross was back in
the centre of her visor, and blasted away.

Exhausted, SID shot out a metal claw and hauled himself onto Ronnie's jet-pack – time to hitch a ride.

As Rocket Ronnie approached the enormous planet of Jupiter, the largest planet in the solar system, the cross on her visor swung to one side yet again.

"Don't tell me ... they've moved off again!" sighed Rocket Ronnie to MAVIS.

"*That's right. My sensors indicate that they're now somewhere near Mars,*" MAVIS replied.

By the time Ronnie had reached Mars, they'd moved again!

"Plundering Pluto! This is getting ridiculous," she said. "It's like trying to catch chickens in a playground. Where are they now?"

"*The moon*," said MAVIS, with a hint of urgency in her voice.

"Earth's moon?" asked Ronnie.

"*Yes*," said MAVIS. "*Whatever they are, they're getting too close for comfort.*"

Rocket Ronnie, with SID on her back, set off towards the small, pale grey orb of the moon. When they arrived, Rocket Ronnie was relieved to see that the cross stayed at the centre of her visor. It seemed these beings hadn't suddenly chosen to disappear somewhere else this time.

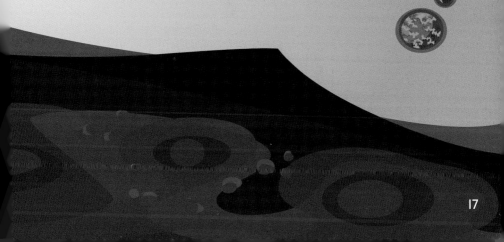

Rocket Ronnie cut her blasters down to a gentle hiss and slowly descended into a crater near to the beings' location. "We need to take care," she whispered to SID. "We don't want to scare them off. We'll sneak up slowly and see what they look like and what they are doing." With a low whistle, SID rolled off Ronnie's jet-pack and bobbed silently at her side.

Rocket Ronnie carefully made her way up the side of the crater and peeped over the edge. There in front of her was a swirling mass of grey cloud. The cloud slowly separated into three smaller clouds, which then took on the form of three figures – like three smoky grey ghosts. They hung in space, silent and still.

"I wonder what they're doing here?" said Rocket Ronnie to herself.

In the distance was a large planet which seemed to be of great interest to these figures. It was Planet Earth.

Rocket Ronnie decided that the most sensible thing to do would be to go up to these figures and simply ask them what they were up to. She wasn't going to find out much by sneaking around and hiding from them.

She scrambled over the edge of the crater and made her way towards them.

"Er, excuse me?" she said. "Hi, I'm Rocket Ronnie. I'm from Earth, the planet you're looking at. I hope you don't mind me asking but ... what are you doing here?"

The three figures billowed slightly and lost their form for a moment, as if they were slightly disturbed by the arrival of this stranger. Rocket Ronnie heard a rather spooky hissing sound, and the hisses became whispered words.

"Go away," said the figures, rather rudely. "We don't want you here. We are busy."

"Busy doing what?" Rocket Ronnie asked.

"Mind your own business," came the hissing reply.

"Well, *excuse me*," exclaimed Rocket Ronnie angrily, putting her hands on her hips, "but this *is* my business, actually. After all, I *am* the Defender of the Human Race."

"We see," said a whispering hiss. "Very well. We'll tell you what you wish to know. Then you can leave us in peace."

"We are the Bleekoids," hissed one of the forms. It was larger than the other two and Rocket Ronnie assumed that it was the leader. "We have searched through this solar system for the perfect planet. The big blue one was too big and cold and mostly made out of gases."

"I think that would be Neptune," said Rocket Ronnie, helpfully.

"The one with a ring of rocks around it –"

"Saturn," interrupted Ronnie.

"Well, whatever it's called, it wasn't any good," continued the Bleekoid, "and the big colourful one was too stormy."

"That'll be Jupiter," guessed Ronnie.

"However, this one ..." hissed the head Bleekoid, pointing a wispy finger at the distant Earth, "... this one is just right!"

Rocket Ronnie grinned – she couldn't help thinking about the story of *Goldilocks and the Three Bears*, although the three Bleekoids, with their hissy voices and ghostly forms, were very unbear-like. "Just right for what?" she asked.

"Just right for development!" hissed the figure.

"Development?" Rocket Ronnie exclaimed. "But Earth is already developed! It has cities and shops and hospitals, as well as natural things like hills and grass and trees."

"Well, we're not interested in those things. They're of no use to us," explained the Bleekoid. "You see, we are business-beings. We intend to build an intergalactic space highway through this solar system so all sorts of space trucks and lorries can get from one side of the galaxy to the other.

"This planet you call Earth will make a perfect stopping-off point – a place where the drivers can take a break, have a snack and refuel. We'll concrete over all the cities and hills and trees and grass. In fact we'll concrete over the whole planet and start again. We'll build fuel stations and fast-food restaurants, and a few shops too. They can sell all sorts of rubbish that people don't really need. It doesn't take much to convince them that they do – we're good at that sort of thing."

"I bet you are!" said Rocket Ronnie through her teeth. She held up a gloved finger and pointed it at the ghostly figure. "Now you listen to me. There are people living on that planet, billions of them, and they don't need more rubbish."

"Yes, we know!" interrupted the Bleekoid. "Don't you concern yourself about them. They will be looked after.

Every human will be issued with a smart uniform. They will be paid, although not very much, and they will be put to work, washing and refuelling the space lorries and serving in the fast-food restaurants and shops."

"They will do no such thing!" yelled Rocket Ronnie. "You will not concrete over Earth and you will not employ the human race on low wages. You will leave this solar system now, and you will never return. Do you understand?"

"And who's going to make us do this?" questioned the Bleekoid.

"I AM!" shouted Rocket Ronnie.

This made all three Bleekoids laugh long and hard.

"Right. Are you willing to leave this solar system peacefully?" asked Rocket Ronnie.

"No!" hissed the three Bleekoids in unison. "Then you leave me no choice!" said Rocket Ronnie.

She flew up into the air, blasted off in a wide, sweeping curve to build up speed ...

... then shot herself like a cannonball right at the three figures.

She passed straight through them and skidded across the lunar surface, tumbling and bumping to a halt.

Feeling slightly bruised, she turned to look back at the Bleekoids. They had turned into a hazy cloud for a moment, then re-formed into the three figures again – three figures who were laughing even louder than before.

"You cannot hurt us, you fool," hissed the leader. "You cannot even touch us. We are made of material beyond your understanding. Now be gone, you annoying child! Go and warn the people of your so-called Planet Earth. Tell them to prepare for re-development!"

Rocket Ronnie wasn't ready to give up so easily. "SID," she said, getting to her feet. "Run a scan over our visitors, please. I want to know exactly what they're made of."

SID opened a slit in his shell and projected a thin red beam of light at the Bleekoids. The head Bleekoid suddenly turned and shot a grey bolt at SID which engulfed him like a cloud. SID let out a slow buzzing noise and then fell silent. He bobbed listlessly for a moment, then sank down to the ground.

"What have you done to SID?" exclaimed Ronnie.

"We've switched him off – the nosey tin can," sneered the Bleekoid.

Luckily, SID had time to send the information collected by the beam to MAVIS before the Bleekoids turned him off.

"Dust," said MAVIS, firmly.

"Dust?" said Rocket Ronnie, quizzically.

"Yes. I'm not sure what sort of dust, but basically they are made up of millions of tiny little particles which are just like dust particles. That's why they can change their form so easily. It's also what they've used to disable SID. The poor thing is clogged up with dust."

"Thanks, MAVIS." Rocket Ronnie was already deep in thought. "I think your information will prove very useful indeed." She drummed her fingers on the bottom of her visor, where her chin would be, and thought some more.

Dust ... eh?

Meanwhile, the Bleekoids ignored her and went back to staring at Earth and muttering to each other about their wretched plan.

"MAVIS," whispered Rocket Ronnie so the
Bleekoids couldn't hear her. "Have we
got any weapons we could use on these
Bleekoid folk? Nothing that will hurt them
– just something to scare them away?"

"*Negative,*" said MAVIS. "*If they were made of something solid, then maybe – but they are just dust-like particles! It's a tricky situation. Any other ideas?*"

Rocket Ronnie thought and thought. "Got it!" she said finally.

"Please be quiet!" said one of the Bleekoids. "We're trying to make our plans over here."

"Can you zap me back to Earth, to the garage at my house?" whispered Ronnie to MAVIS.

"*I'm setting the co-ordinates right now,*" replied MAVIS, in an equally quiet voice.

"Good. Give me thirty seconds and then zap me back to this exact spot," said Ronnie.

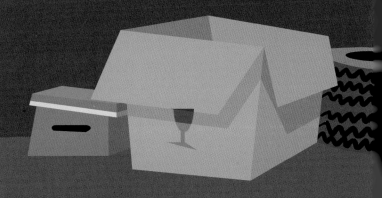

A moment later, in a flash of white light, Rocket Ronnie appeared in the garage at her house. It was strange to be at home all dressed up in her spacesuit and helmet. She hoped her mum wouldn't suddenly come in and find her there.

As quickly as she could, she searched the shelves and cupboards.

"Where is it? Where is it? Why does Dad have to leave this place in such a mess?" she muttered to herself. Finally she found what she was looking for, and just in time. A moment later the whole garage lit up with a flash of white light and Ronnie was gone.

Rocket Ronnie reappeared back on the moon – this time with something hidden behind her back.

"Er, hello again," said Ronnie, stepping over to where the Bleekoids were hissing their plans to each other like a nest of snakes. "Can we have a chat about something?"

"You!" hissed the leader. "I thought we'd seen the last of you, you troublesome little tyke. What do you want now?"

"I just want to ask you one last time. Will you leave our solar system peacefully and never come back?" said Rocket Ronnie.

"And I will answer you one last time," the leader hissed. "No. Now GO AWAY!"

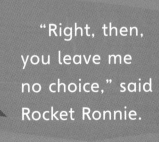

"Right, then, you leave me no choice," said Rocket Ronnie.

She pulled the contraption from behind her back and switched it on. It let out a whining noise as she waved it in front of the three Bleekoids.

"Aaaargh!" cried the Bleekoids. The whine slowly turned into a very satisfying roar as each and every one of the particles that made up the Bleekoids' ghostly forms were quickly pulled into the device in Rocket Ronnie's hand.

She swung the device around to make sure that she hadn't missed any bits of the ghostly trouble-makers and, when she was sure that they had completely vanished, Rocket Ronnie switched off the machine.

Aaaargh!

"Let us out!" came a muffled cry from inside the machine.

"Now why would I want to do that?" Rocket Ronnie replied.

"Because we want you to!" bleated the trapped Bleekoids.

"Because you want me to," repeated Ronnie, thoughtfully. "Well, I must say, there are things that I want too. In fact I'm sure everyone on Planet Earth wants them, but you seemed happy to ignore these things before I put you in this comfy little box."

"We won't ignore them now," cried the Bleekoids, pathetically.

"Good. Well, I want you to leave our solar system and never, ever return. Do you agree?" asked Ronnie.

"Yes, yes! Whatever you say!" they wailed. "Just let us out!"

"And what's the magic word?" asked Rocket Ronnie, rather enjoying herself.

"PLEASE!" howled the Bleekoids in desperation.

"Oh, and I want all that dust taken out of my friend too. I want him back to normal," said Ronnie.

"Yes, all right ... whatever!" moaned the Bleekoids.

whatever...

With SID under her arm, Rocket Ronnie blasted up into space. When she was a good distance from the moon, she opened up her gadget and shook the particles out into the eternal darkness. The particles quickly formed into a cloud. A thin line of dusty grey spiralled out from SID and joined the cloud. Then the cloud quickly flew away, far off into the distance, never to return.

Pleased and relieved, Rocket Ronnie watched it go. Then she looked down at her small metal friend. "Are you all right?" she asked.

SID let out a happy squeak to show that he was completely back to normal.

"Good," said Rocket Ronnie. "Job done! Let's get back to the space station!"

Both Rocket Ronnie and SID were greeted by MAVIS's cool, calm voice as they arrived back at the station. *"A satisfactory outcome,"* she said. *"You've done it again Rocket Ronnie – you've saved the human race. What is that amazing gadget you used on those Bleekoids?"*

"This?" said Rocket Ronnie, looking at the small machine she held in her hand. "Oh, it's a mini vacuum cleaner. My dad uses it to clean out his car at weekends," she grinned.

"*Simple, but remarkably effective!*" laughed MAVIS, and SID hooted and bleeped in agreement.

"Well, I had better get back to Planet Earth. I'm going to be late for school."

"*Yes, of course, Rocket Ronnie,*" said MAVIS. "*See you next time Planet Earth is in danger.*"

"You bet," said Rocket Ronnie. "Goodbye, MAVIS." She patted her little silver companion. "Goodbye, SID."

Moments later, Rocket Ronnie felt the now familiar tingling sensation spread through her body.

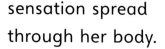

As the rushing and roaring sound engulfed her, she shut her eyes tight for the sudden journey home.

The next thing she knew, she was standing in the alley between the two houses, dressed in her everyday clothes – plain old Veronica Witworth again, and still holding the mini vacuum cleaner in her hand. "Who would have thought that Planet Earth would be saved by something as simple as this?" she said to herself, putting the vacuum cleaner into her school bag.

She went and found her bike, which was still chained to the lamp post, and unlocked it. For a moment, she looked over at what was left of her field. Just a muddy mess from the comings and goings of the trucks and lorries.

"Goodbye, field," she said, sadly. "I suppose there are some things even a superhero can't save." Then she cycled off to school.

"Hello, Veronica," said her teacher, looking at his watch when Veronica finally arrived. "Where have you been?"

"Sorry I'm late, Mr Green," said Veronica, unable to hide her smile. "There was something I needed to clear up."